W9-BOC-440

Paddington Bear

PADDINGTON BEAR
Text copyright © 1972 by Michael Bond
Illustrations copyright © 1992 by HarperCollins Publishers Ltd.
First published in Great Britain by William Collins Sons and Co Ltd.
This edition published in 1992 by HarperCollins Publishers Ltd.
Printed and bound in the People's Republic of China.
All rights reserved.
1 2 3 4 5 6 7 8 9 10
First American Edition, 1992

Library of Congress Cataloging-in-Publication Data
Bond, Michael.
    Paddington bear / Michael Bond ; illustrated by John Lobban.
       p.   cm.
    Summary: While waiting for their daughter Judy to arrive at
Paddington Station, Mr. and Mrs. Brown spot a small bear, recently
arrived from darkest Peru, and take him home to join their family.
    ISBN 0-694-00394-8
    [1. Bears—Fiction.] I. Lobban, John, ill. II. Title.
PZ7.B6368Pach   1992   91-29781
                                                          CIP
                                                           AC

Paddington Bear

Michael Bond

Illustrated by John Lobban

HarperCollins*Publishers*

One day Mr. and Mrs. Brown were standing in Paddington Station. They were waiting for their daughter Judy who was coming home from school. Suddenly Mr. Brown noticed something small and furry behind a pile of mailbags.

"Look over there," he said to Mrs. Brown, "I'm sure I saw a bear."

"A *bear*?" said Mrs. Brown. "In Paddington Station? Don't be silly, Henry. There can't be."

But there was. It had a funny kind of hat and it was sitting all by itself on an old suitcase near the Lost Property Office.

As they drew near, the bear stood up and politely raised its hat. "Good afternoon," it said, in a small clear voice. "Can I help you?"

"We were wondering if *we* could help *you*," said

Mrs. Brown. "Where ever have you come from?"

The bear looked around carefully before replying. "Darkest Peru. I stowed away and I lived on marmalade!"

Mrs. Brown spied a label around the bear's neck. It said simply:

"Henry," she exclaimed, "we will have to take him home with us."

"But we don't even know his name," began Mr. Brown.

"We'll call him Paddington," said Mrs. Brown. "Because that's where we found him."

Mrs. Brown went off to look for Judy while Mr.
Brown took Paddington to the restaurant for something to eat.

He left Paddington sitting at a corner table near the
window. He soon returned carrying two steaming
cups of tea and a large plate piled high with
desserts.

After his long journey Paddington felt so hungry and thirsty he didn't know which to do first—eat or drink.

"I think I'll try both at the same time if you don't mind, Mr. Brown," he announced. And without waiting for a reply he climbed up onto the table. Mr. Brown stared out of the window, pretending he had tea with a bear at Paddington Station every day of his life.

When Mrs. Brown came into the restaurant with Judy, she threw up her hands in horror.

"Henry," she said. "What are you doing to that poor bear? He's covered all over with cream and jam."

At the sound of Mrs. Brown's voice Paddington jumped so much he stepped on a patch of strawberry jam and fell over backward into his cup of tea.

"I think we'd better go before anything else happens," said Mr. Brown. And he quickly led the way out of the restaurant.

Judy took Paddington's paw and squeezed it.

"Come along," she said. "We'll take you home in a taxi. Then you can take a nice, hot bath and meet my brother Jonathan."

Paddington had never been in a taxi before. He found it very exciting, and he stood on a little folding seat behind the driver so that he could wave to the people in the street.

Soon they pulled up outside a large house with a green front door.

When they were inside, Judy took Paddington up to his room to unpack.

"I haven't got very much," said Paddington. "Only some marmalade . . .

and my scrapbook . . .

and a South American penny."

He held up a photo-graph. "And that is my Aunt Lucy. She had it taken just before she went into the Home for Retired Bears."

Next Judy showed Paddington to the bathroom.

As soon as he was on his own he turned on the faucets and then climbed onto a stool in order to look out of the window.

Then he tried writing his name on the steamy glass with his paw. It took him quite a long time, and when he looked round, he found to his surprise that the bath was so full of water it was starting to run over the side.

He closed his eyes and, holding his nose with one paw, he jumped in.

The water was hot, soapy, and very deep, and to his horror he found he couldn't get out. He couldn't even see to turn the faucets off.

Paddington tried calling out "Help," at first in a quiet voice so as not to disturb anyone, and then much louder, "HELP! HELP!"

But still nobody came.

Then he had an idea.

He took off his hat and began using it to bail out the water.

Downstairs, Judy was telling her brother all about Paddington.

Suddenly, she felt a PLOP.

Looking up she saw a dark, wet patch on the ceiling.

"Paddington," she cried. "He must be in trouble. Quick!"

And together they raced up the stairs.

Jonathan and Judy leaned over the side of the bath and lifted a dripping and very frightened Paddington out of the tub.

"What a mess!" said Jonathan. "We'd better wipe it up pretty quickly."

"Oh Paddington," said Judy. "I'm so glad we found you in time. You could have drowned."

Paddington sat up. "I'm glad I had my hat," he said.

Later on, a beautifully clean Paddington came downstairs. Settling himself into a small armchair by the fire, he put his paws behind his head and stretched out his toes.

It was nice being a bear—especially a bear called Paddington. He had a feeling that life with the Browns was going to be fun.